Tellwell Talent
www.tellwell.ca

ISBN
978-0-2288-6675-6 (Hardcover)
978-0-2288-6673-2 (Paperback)
978-0-2288-6674-9 (eBook)

You're not a Chicken

Mark Goring

Once upon a time there was an eagle's nest in an oak tree right above a chicken coop.

A storm came, and a strong wind tipped the eagle's nest. An egg rolled out of the eagle's nest and fell gently into a chicken nest.

Not too long after, all the eggs in the chicken nest hatched.

Would you believe that the little eagle grew up thinking he was a chicken?

He learned to act just like a chicken because he thought he was a chicken. He walked like a chicken, he ate like a chicken, he talked like a chicken.

Sometimes he even thought like a chicken.

Occasionally an eagle would fly by and would notice something strange: an eagle in the chicken coop.

The kind eagle would land on a post and say: "What are you doing in here?

You're not a chicken, you're an eagle! You can fly. You're not meant to be in a chicken coop." The little eagle would respond by saying: "You don't know what you're talking about. I'm a chicken. I always was a chicken, and I always will be a chicken."

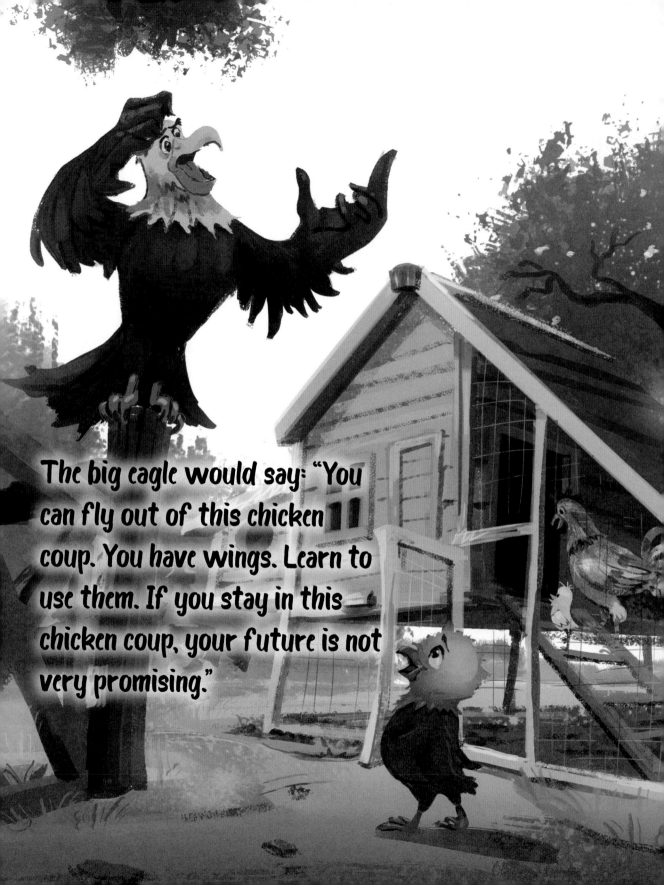

The big eagle would say: "You can fly out of this chicken coup. You have wings. Learn to use them. If you stay in this chicken coup, your future is not very promising."

The little eagle thought that what the eagle was saying was nonsense and yet deep inside the little eagle did feel that he could fly.

Sometimes he would even flap his wings a little and try to fly but the chickens would laugh at him and tell him: "Why are you trying to fly? You're a chicken and chickens can't fly!"

The little eagle went on living like a chicken, but he wasn't happy.

Deep inside the little eagle there was something that longed to fly like the eagles.

One day in desperation, he decided he didn't care what the other chickens thought about him so with all his might he began to flap his wings.

And low and behold, this little eagle lifted off the ground and flew over the fence and above the oak and into the big blue sky.

Finally, the little eagle knew that he wasn't a chicken. He was an eagle, and he could fly.

Made in the USA
Middletown, DE
01 April 2022

63495853R00015